SPIRITUALLY CORRECT BEDTIME STORIES

PARABLES OF FAITH FOR THE MODERN READER

CHRIS FABRY

InterVarsity Press
Downers Grove, Illinois

InterVarsity Press® is the book-publishing division of InterVarsity Christian Fellowship®, a student movement active on campus at hundreds of universities, colleges and schools of nursing in the United States of America, and a member movement of the International Fellowship of Evangelical Students. For information about local and regional activities, write Public Relations Dept., InterVarsity Christian Fellowship, 6400 Schroeder Rd., P.O. Box 7895, Madison, WI 53707-7895.

Cover illustration: Kurt Mitchell
Illuminated letters: Don Frye

ISBN 0-8308-1955-X

Printed in the United States of America ♾

Library of Congress Cataloging-in-Publication Data

Fabry, Chris, 1961-
   Spiritually correct bedtime stories: parables of faith for the
modern reader/Chris Fabry.

     p.   cm.
   ISBN 0-8308-1955-X (hc: alk. paper)
   1. Christian fiction, American.   2. Humorous stories, American.
3. Fairy tales—adaptations. 4. Parables. I. Title.
PS3556.A26S67   1995
813'54—dc20   *95-19131*
                                                      CIP

15	14	13	12	11	10	9	8	7	6	5	4	3	2	1
07	06	05	04	03	02	01	00	99	98	97	96	95		

*For my mother, who read to me
and gave the gift of laughter,
and for all who do the same.*

Introduction

If you're in the mood to look in the mirror and laugh, you've picked up the right book. Somewhere between puberty and the first mortgage we tend to lose that ability to smile at ourselves. I'm not sure why. Maybe we need a bigger mirror.

People of faith are particularly wary of too much laughing, often because we think it's childish. Of course there's quite a difference between being child-*ish* and being child*like*. It's childish to whine when you don't get your way or fret about things you have no control over. But it is childlike to laugh from your toes. It's childlike to trust so much that you slip your hand into your father's and skip down the sidewalk. These stories should be taken in with such wonder.

Some will no doubt read too much into them or try to read between the lines. Please resist the urge. Have fun. Skip through the pages like a child.

If you do happen to come away with a deep, life-changing truth, I will rejoice. I'll also be happy to hear that you stopped several times because your blood pressure rises when you chuckle. I'm sure there's medication for that.

For those who simply must know where I'm coming from, I own several study Bibles, we've educated our kids at home and in public schools, I vote regularly and think we should be involved in the political process, I love Christian publishers, I believe prophecy and angels are important for biblical study, I support seeker and traditional churches alike, I love traditional hymns and praise choruses, and I know many who have found personal comfort and help from Christian psychologists.

What you see reflected in these tales are extremes. It's a broad-brush view of the issues and movements we find in Christian circles today.

There is a Latin phrase that beautifully sums up what I want you to learn from these tales. Unfortunately I didn't do well in Latin, and I won't ask someone who did because I'm an American male. I think it's something like *Carpe Smilem,* but I'll probably never know for sure. Sorry. Enjoy them anyway.

THE THREE
THEOLOGICAL PIGS

nce upon a time there were three pigs who lived in a house with their devout mother.

One day she said to her children, "You have learned all you can from Sunday school. It is time you went on for deeper study." So the three pigs packed their bags and applied to a fine seminary. Alas, only one pig was actually accepted, so the other two settled for a correspondence course.

After a time, the three pigs started their ministries. The first met a man with a load of straw theology. "Please, sir," he said, "will you give me some to build my church?"

"Certainly," said the man, and he also gave the pig a sign that said, "Miracles Galore Tonight."

Quick as a wink the first pig's church went up, and a large congregation was attracted to each service. The little pig promised healing, prosperity and more pleasing snouts for everyone. Little did he know it was the big, bad wolf who had actually given him the straw. The wolf lurked in the narthex, watching the pig's success.

The little pig was about to start an "Oinking in the Spirit" service when he heard a knock on his study door.

"Little pig, little pig, let me in," said the wolf. "I want to contribute to the building program."

"Well, come right in," said the little pig. But when he saw it was a wolf he turned his curly tail, splashed through the baptistery and headed for his brother's church.

Meanwhile, the second pig had met a man who was carrying a load of sticks. This of course was also the wolf, who had many disguises and more building materials than you could—yes, shake a stick at.

"Please, sir," said the little pig, "will you give me some of that kindling to build my church?"

The wolf agreed and gave suggestions to the little

pig for a really big turnout at Sunday's praise service.

As quick as two winks, the second pig built his church, complete with a massive parking lot. Then he built an Olympic-sized swimming pool, an ice rink, basketball courts and a sanctuary with stained glass, and he thanked his Creator for allowing him to do it all on credit. He was in one of the community rooms leading a "Swines Anonymous" twelve-step program when his brother came bursting through the door.

"You've got to help me!" the first little pig exclaimed.

"Sit down," said his brother, "and we'll help you deal with your pain."

"You don't understand. There's a big, bad wolf chasing me, and he's coming this way."

"I'm glad you're facing your fears," said the brother. "The first step is always admitting you have a problem."

Suddenly they heard a knock at the door.

"Don't let him fool you with the building program line," said the first little pig.

"Who is it?" called the brother.

"Little pigs, let me in," said the wolf. "I'm in need of counseling."

The brother immediately opened the door and gave the wolf his hourly rate.

"Silly pig," the wolf growled, "the only counseling I'll need is Overeaters Anonymous, because I'm going to gobble up you both."

The wolf did just that and felt very proud of the accomplishment. Then, since wolves are not at all shame-based, he picked himself up and headed over to eat the third pig.

When he got there, he peeked into an old shack and saw the pig kneeling. The pig was gaunt from hunger, for he had been fasting. Furthermore, the little pig had spent many years and much money in seminary and had only a tiny bit of money for food.

Feeling quite full, the wolf sat down outside the window and listened.

"And please," the pig prayed, "please keep the few pigs we have in the congregation unspotted from the world, and keep me true to my first love."

Wearying of the pig's prayers, the wolf set out to eat him, bony as he was. He tapped lightly on the door and whispered, "Little pig, little pig, where is your church building, and what time are your Sunday services?"

The little pig stopped praying and said, "We have

no building, friend. We meet in the wee schoolhouse on the corner and can afford only an eleven-o'clock worship."

"If you'll come out," said the crafty wolf, "I will contribute enough for two buildings."

"It is written," the little pig said: " 'Why should I fear when wicked deceivers surround me—those who trust in their wealth and boast of their great riches?' "

"And who are you to touch one anointed from on high?" scoffed the wolf. "Open the door and you will see how much I can bless you."

Because of his discerning spirit, the little pig refused to accept the wolf's invitation.

Filled with rage, the wolf yelled, "Little pig, let me in, or I'll huff and I'll puff and I'll blow holes in your theology!"

" 'The grass withers and the flowers fall, but the word of the Lord stands forever,' "

The wolf tried to climb into the shack through the window, but he slipped and fell, and his bulging stomach burst and the two little pigs popped out.

"Thank you, brother," said the pigs.

"I've been praying you would visit our church someday," said the third pig, "but I never thought you'd arrive like this!"

And the pigs talked and wept, repented and forgave, and prayed together. To this day they are ministering mightily in a very small congregation upwind of the sty.

THE THREE HOLY GOATS GRUFF

igh on a lush hillside in a deep green pasture there lived three Holy Goats Gruff. They spent their days in harmony and fellowship, having potluck praise-and-prayer suppers and enjoying creation.

At the foot of the hill lay a wide, deep stream and a bridge they had not crossed in many years. Underneath the bridge lived a horrible, mean, nasty, worldly troll who, as it was told in those parts, was a card-carrying member of several liberal organizations. He referred to the goats as "those fundamentalists" and was bent on keeping the holy goats separated from society.

On the other side of the stream was a rocky slope covered with dangerous crags. The forlorn animals that stumbled about on these rocks did not enjoy creation like the Holy Goats Gruff did, because they did not know their Creator.

The Holy Goats Gruff were so busy with dinners and the fun they were having that they didn't think about the other side of the stream. They were content with their little slice of heavenly pasture.

But one day the littlest Holy Goat Gruff, who had a particularly sensitive conscience, spoke up. "This morning I was thinking about the good things we enjoy every day and how lighthearted we are with the bounty we possess," he said. "But when I looked on the other side of the stream I saw despondent and dejected animals. I believe we need to cross the bridge and tell others what we have found."

"What about the horrible, mean, card-carrying troll?" the Middle Holy Goat Gruff said.

"We'll invite him too," the Little Holy Goat Gruff said innocently.

"We're behind you," the Big Holy Goat Gruff said. "Lead the way."

Little Holy Goat Gruff went trip-trapping across the bridge with his little hoofs.

"Who's making that confounded noise on my bridge?" said the troll, exiting his computer's liberal on-line forum.

"It is I, Little Holy Goat Gruff," said the goat in his wee small voice. "I have come to help restore a sense of morality in a society plagued with ills. I have chosen the political arena to make a difference."

"Oh no you're not," roared the troll. "I am coming up to eat you!"

Little Holy Goat Gruff was afraid. "Oh, please don't eat me," he said. "Wait for my big brother. He is much more conservative and is much larger and tastier than I am. Anyway, what can a little goat like me do in such a world as this?"

"Good point," the troll said, licking his lips. "I wouldn't want to waste my appetite on a scrawny kid like you. Besides, you're too young to vote. Go ahead and cross."

So Little Holy Goat Gruff crossed the bridge safely and engaged the culture on the other side.

Then Middle Holy Goat Gruff's middle-sized hoofs came clomping across the wooden bridge.

"Who's that clomping over my bridge?" called the troll.

"It is I, Middle Holy Goat Gruff," said the goat in

his middle-sized voice.

"Don't you know there's a separation between church and state?" the troll roared. "I am coming up to eat you!"

Middle Holy Goat Gruff was afraid and thought about turning back. But he saw his younger brother encouraging him from the other side, so he stood his ground.

"I have a right to go on that side of the stream like anyone else," he said. "I am going into education to touch lives by teaching truth to young minds."

"No you aren't!" screamed the troll. "We can't have your kind imposing your morality and inflicting your values on our children! You'll think you have a right to sit on the school board. I'm going to start gobbling if you don't scram."

Middle Holy Goat Gruff shook with fear and said, "Please don't eat me. Wait for my big brother. He is tastier, much more conservative, and has a Rush Limbaugh figure."

"Hmmm," said the troll, "that *would* be a good meal. I don't want to spoil my appetite on you. Just make sure you don't use the word *God* or bring a Bible to class. That really gets my goat."

So Middle Holy Goat Gruff crossed the bridge safely and secured a teaching position at the local high school on the other side.

Then Big Holy Goat Gruff stepped onto the bridge. Its planks sagged under his weight, and with each hoofstep the whole bridge shook.

"Who is that sagging the planks on my bridge?" roared the troll in his loudest voice.

"It is I, Big Holy Goat Gruff," the goat shouted.

"I suppose you're going to tell me to wait for your big brother," said the troll.

"No, I am the biggest one there is," said Big Holy Goat Gruff. "I am on my way to law school to right injustice and learn how to write a friend-of-the-court brief."

"Oh no you're not!" bellowed the troll. "You have no right meddling in laws on this side of the stream. Go back to your lush hillside, or I'll come up to eat you!"

"Come on up," said Big Holy Goat Gruff. "I am ready to meet you."

The troll climbed onto the bridge and rushed at Big Holy Goat Gruff. To his surprise the goat was sitting on the bridge looking very placid.

"What in the world are you doing?" roared the troll.

"I am staging a nonviolent protest against your anti-free-speech bullying," said Big Holy Goat Gruff.

Standing beside the goat was a man who produced a piece of paper. "I am legal counsel for the three clients known as H. G. Gruff," said this man, a lawyer from Concerned Mammals of America. "This is a restraining order for you to cease and desist your unlawful actions against them."

The troll was so angry that he sent several press releases to his colleagues in the media, but to no avail. Finally he jumped into the icy waters and disappeared beneath the flood.

After that the three Holy Goats Gruff crossed the bridge whenever they liked and brought many fellow animals over to the lush green hillside. They remained true to their convictions of restoring virtue and values to the land and were good examples to everyone.

The horrible mean troll resurfaced downstream and started a lobby against the goats and their kind. But to this day the Holy Goats Gruff remain steadfast in their pursuit of justice, and they pray daily that the troll will turn from his ways and join them in the quiet pasture.

CHICKEN LITTLE

hicken Little was picking up corn in the barnyard one bright sunny day. The wind ruffled her feathers and turned the pages of the magazine she was reading, *Today's Christian Chicken*. Suddenly, an object fell from above and clunked her on the head.

Chicken Little dropped her corn and magazine and looked up. She could see trees swaying, and it seemed to her the sky was falling.

Then she looked behind her and saw the object, a long piece of folded paper. "Dear me," she clucked. "I wonder what it is."

Soon she discovered she was holding a copy of a

new bill to be passed in Congress that very day. Though it seemed innocent, it had an obscure provision that left the door open for barn-based health clinics.

"Oh my," she clucked. "This is worse than the sky falling."

As Chicken Little ran past the big red barn, she met her friend Henny Penny, who was watching over the church day-care center.

"Why, Chicken Little, where are you going in such a hurry?" cackled Henny Penny.

"Oh dear, haven't you heard about the new bill? It will bring a new agenda to the barnyard. I am going to complain to the king!"

"Oh, Chicken Little, how do you know that?" asked Henny Penny.

"I saw it and I read it and I've been afraid this would happen all along!" clucked Chicken Little.

"I'll come with you, Chicken Little," cackled Henny Penny, and she put a *McChick and Me* video in the VCR and left her class peeping happily.

They ran past the barn and various pieces of farm machinery. Soon they met Cocky Locky, who was forever preening himself for his spiritual accomplishments.

"Well, where are you two going in such a hurry?" cackled Cocky Locky.

"Oh dear, today Congress is voting on a new bill that will surely change the farm. I think it will ban all religious speech or something, and we are going to complain to the king," said Henny Penny.

"How do you know that?" asked Cocky Locky in wonderment.

"Chicken Little told me!"

"Then let's catch up with her and tell the king!" crowed Cocky Locky. "I have a personal friend in the cabinet."

Soon they came to the edge of the pond. There was Groggy Froggy sunning himself in the mud. "Hello," he said. "Why are you running so fast on such a warm day?"

"Oh dear, Groggy Froggy, a new bill in Congress will ban anything Christian in print, on television, on radio and even in our church, so we're going to tell the king!" Cocky Locky crowed. "You know how successful I've been at defeating the liberal lobby."

"But how do you know there's such a bill?" ribbeted Groggy Froggy.

Cocky Locky said, "Henny Penny told me."

Henny Penny said, "Chicken Little told me."

"My, my," said Groggy Froggy as he jumped from his bed of mud. "Wait for me. I'll come too." And he hopped along after them.

At the other end of the pond, Lucille Goose (who did not like to be called "Loosey") was teaching her goslings to honk in tongues. She looked up and saw the animals running down the lane.

"Where are you going?" she said.

"Oh dear, a bill is passing," ribbeted Groggy Froggy importantly, "and it will take away our belief in God, and we're going to complain to the king."

"But who told you that a bill is passing?" asked Lucille.

"Cocky Locky told me," said Groggy Froggy.

"Henny Penny told me," said Cocky Locky.

"Chicken Little told me!" said Henny Penny.

Chicken Little said, "I saw it and I read it and I've been afraid this would happen all along. And now we're going straight to the authorities."

"Wait for me," honked Lucille Goose, and flapping her big wings madly, she ran down the lane after them.

They came to a path in the woods, and there they met Waily Quaily, who was always crying about something. "Why are you all coming after me?" asked Waily Quaily defensively.

"We're not coming after you," honked Lucille Goose. "A bill is passing that will compel us to hire foxes in the henhouse, and we're going to complain to the king."

"That's not half as bad as the movie I'm protesting," whined Waily Quaily. "It's really terrible."

"Have you seen it yet?" asked Chicken Little.

"No, but I just know it's terrible and will be the end of the barnyard as we know it. I'll go with you and we can protest together."

So the whole group headed toward the castle of the king—but soon they came upon Foxy Woxy.

"Where are all you fine folks going in such a hurry?" asked Foxy Woxy.

"A bill is passing and a bad movie is being made," said Chicken Little. "We are going to let our voices be heard."

"Why don't you just start a letter-writing campaign?" said Foxy Woxy. "You could send faxes and telegrams and jam the king's switchboard with calls of outrage."

"Oh dear," clucked Chicken Little. "Why didn't we think of that earlier?"

"If you'll come over to my cave," Foxy Woxy said invitingly, "I'll give you access to my media center and you can set up your headquarters there."

Everyone agreed to the blitz. Foxy Woxy went ahead, and the others followed in line. They were almost to his home when they met Wordy Birdy.

"What a lovely day for a walk," she called. "May I ask where you are going?"

"Oh dear, a bill is passing," said Chicken Little, "and a terrible movie is being made. We're all going to speak our mind to the king and let him know how powerful we are against these terrible developments."

"And how do you know a bill is passing?" asked Wordy Birdy.

"Because I saw it and I read it and I've been afraid this would happen all along."

"May I see a copy of the legislation?" asked Wordy Birdy.

Chicken Little handed her a photocopy, and Wordy Birdy clicked her tongue against her beak. "Oh dear," she said.

"What's the matter?" said Cocky Locky. "Don't you think we have enough clout to stop it? I have a friend in the cabinet, you know."

"My chicks are in danger!" said Henny Penny.

"My geese are cooked if this goes through," said Lucille Goose.

"Everyone's against me," whined Waily Quaily.

"We've got to get to the phones and faxes now," barked Foxy Woxy.

In her wise way, Wordy Birdy motioned with her wing for them to stop. "This is simply a photocopy of the same bill that's been distributed for years and years," said she. "It's not real."

"And what about the movie?" whined Waily Quaily.

"Again, it's a rumor that's run around here for quite some time."

"Then we got all worked up for nothing?" asked Chicken Little.

"I'm afraid so," said Wordy Birdy. "Your heavenly Father knows your frame and understands. Who of you by worrying can add a single hour to your life? As a matter of fact, you will surely be eaten if you continue on this path."

So Chicken Little, Henny Penny, Cocky Locky, Groggy Froggy, Waily Quaily and Lucille Goose ran back to the barnyard.

As Wordy Birdy flew away, she noticed Foxy Woxy shaking his paw at her and lamenting her advice. For it was Foxy Woxy who had planted the bill in the barnyard and spread the movie rumor to strike fear into the animals and make them his noontime feast.

COMPULSIVELLA

nce upon a time there lived a man whose wife died. Jumping into another relationship much too quickly, he married a woman who was mean—and her two daughters were worse. So he spent most of his time at work or sitting in on board meetings at church and being an absentee father.

This caused deep scars for his own kind and lovely daughter Ella. It also meant she bore the brunt of dysfunction in this blended family.

No sooner had the mother and daughters moved in than the stepmother began tearing down what little self-esteem Ella possessed. But the woman did commend Ella's habit of cleaning everything, and this cast the poor girl into an obsession.

Ella washed the dishes, scrubbed the stairs, polished the floors, cleaned the stove and did it all without realizing she was looking for approval. Every night she took her fifteen-minute-meal-for-busy-women container from the freezer for herself, then cooked a balanced dinner for the family.

After washing and drying the dishes, she cleaned cinders from the chimney for further validation. Because of this her stepsisters thought of nicknaming her "Cinderella," but Ella thought this was too beautiful a name for the likes of her. The sisters decided that "Compulsivella" was a better fit.

It happened that the most eligible bachelor in town, the parson's son, invited all the young ladies of the kingdom to a nondenominational church picnic. Whoever baked the tastiest item for dinner would be his bride. The sisters planned their menus and outfits carefully. As a codependent, Compulsivella volunteered her time so she could keep everyone happy.

"Aren't you going to the picnic?" asked the sisters. "You're dressed perfectly for the sack race."

"The parson's son would never marry me," Compulsivella moaned. "I'm so ugly, and besides it's been three weeks since I dusted behind the refrigerator. There's just so much to do."

The long-awaited evening came at last, and the two proud sisters stepped into a beautiful carriage and rode away to the picnic. Alone with her mop, Compulsivella was caught in a mire of negative thinking. To lift her spirits she turned on the radio.

The dial was set to a counseling program, and the host seemed to be talking directly to her. She called his 800 number and was on the air in a matter of minutes.

"Thank you for your call," the man said after listening to her story. "Are you seeing a counselor?"

"I don't deserve one," Compulsivella said. "I can't afford in-patient care, and when I call in to programs like this I wind up cleaning the earpiece on the phone."

"Do not despair," he said gently. "I'll be your fairy therapist. I can help solve all your problems. Now tell me about your childhood."

The fairy therapist soon knew Compulsivella's whole story. Because she used her real name and not "Anonymous," so did the rest of the kingdom.

"I only know what you've told me," said the fairy therapist. "And this advice should not be substituted for professional help, but I think you want to go to the picnic."

"How did you know that?" Compulsivella gasped.

"Trust me," he said. "Go to the garden and get a pumpkin."

Compulsivella wondered how this could possibly help, but she hurried to the garden, brought back the largest organically grown pumpkin, cleaned it off thoroughly and set it on the table.

"This pumpkin represents all your hurtful relationships and the shame of your past," the radio therapist said. "I want you to strike it now and get out your aggression. Feel free to scream through your rage."

Compulsivella did as her fairy therapist said, and soon the pumpkin was pulverized. "That felt pretty good," Compulsivella said. "What do I do now?"

"Bake a pie with what is left and take it to the picnic," the fairy therapist said. "You're a winner! You can do it! And you're very important to me. Now let me put you on hold, we have a commercial break coming."

Compulsivella did not waste any time baking the pie, and what a pie it was. But when the therapist's voice returned, she gave vent to her anxiety: "What will I wear? I have only rags."

"When was the last time you bought something nice for yourself?" the fairy therapist asked.

"I can't remember when," she said.

"Exactly! You wear rags because you think you're not a valuable person. Go out immediately and spend some money on a nice outfit. Tell yourself you are a good person. Get out of the downward cycle and get the spiral going upward.

"But be careful," he warned. "When you hear the clock strike midnight, you must leave because your love tank will need refilling. And don't forget to pay off your credit card quickly, or you'll experience a massive amount of consumer debt."

"How do you know that?" asked Compulsivella.

"I'm also a fairy financial counselor."

"I will pay it off," Compulsivella promised. But when she maxed out her VISA with an expensive dress and shoes, she actually launched the first bout in what would become a long fight with shopaholism.

As she walked toward the picnic grounds, a murmur of admiration fluttered through the crowd. "How striking she is," everyone said.

The parson's son took the pie from her and set her at the place of honor. Since dancing was not allowed, they played a fast game of Uno until the feast was prepared. Because the young man was visually oriented, he hardly touched his meal—so taken was he with Compulsivella's beauty.

When dessert came and the pumpkin pie was served, the clock struck eleven. Compulsivella's breathing became irregular, and she realized she was having a panic attack. She stood up, curtsied and ran away. (She would later discover, during a group session, that her self-esteem was still dangerously low and she was repressing a memory about a faulty alarm clock.)

Soon after she returned home, her stepmother and stepsisters entered. "If you had been to the picnic, you would have seen the most beautiful princess ever," said one sister.

"No one knows her name, but the parson's son is very interested in her," said the other.

Compulsivella was so overjoyed that she put down her security vacuum. The next day the parson's son came riding through the village with the half-eaten pumpkin pie, a pathetic sight indeed.

"If anyone can identify this pie and prove she made it," he shouted through a flood of tears, "I will straightaway marry her, and we shall live happily ever after."

Though Compulsivella heard the call, she was too

wounded and needy to respond. The stepsisters heaped false guilt upon her and asked her to help them make a pie to fool the parson's son. As usual she complied, giving them way too much control. But this second pie was not the same, because Compulsivella had not embraced the pain that led to the creation of the first glorious pie.

The parson's son returned home without the mystery woman. Compulsivella became absorbed with herself, but after a while she went back to her group meetings.

One week she noticed a handsome but poorly dressed young man cowering in the corner of the church basement where the group met. To her surprise it was the parson's son. He was dealing with PDD, Princess Deficit Disorder.

A few months later, the parson performed the wedding ceremony live on the fairy therapist's daily program. Compulsivella and her new husband started a small group ministry and made plans to release their first teaching video.

Since they learned to lower their expectations for each other, they have lived happily ever after, though Compulsivella continues to deal with her credit history and the adverse effects of living with a "messy."

THE LITTLE
RED HEN

iligence and faithfulness were the hallmarks of the Little Red Hen. She lived in a church-sponsored apartment complex that brought together animals from differing ethnic and socioeconomic strata.

The pig, the duck and the cat dwelled with her, but alas, they never did anything for the church. The pig liked to wallow in the mud and recite verses, the duck enjoyed the pond and quacked a few bars of favorite hymns, and the cat purred on the patio in the sunshine.

One day the Little Red Hen found a decision card lying on the ground.

"Who will help me follow up this needy soul?" she asked.

"Not I," grunted the pig from the mud. "I'm working on my memory verse for the week, Proverbs 11:22."

"Not I," quacked the duck from the pond. "I'm only on the third stanza of 'Make Me a Blessing.' " And she sang, "Give as 'twas given to you in your need . . ."

"Not I," purred the cat. "But I'll certainly pray for you."

So the Little Red Hen set off and made contact with the mare who had filled out the decision card. The horse was truly repentant, and so the Little Red Hen began discipling her.

The next week the Little Red Hen was cleaning the house when the pastor called and asked her to teach a Sunday-school class.

"My, but I'm awfully busy," said the Little Red Hen. "But the tiny ones need a teacher desperately. If I can't find someone else, I'll do it."

"Who will help teach Sunday school?" asked the Little Red Hen.

"Not I," yawned the pig. "It's not my spiritual gift."

"Not I," quacked the duck. "I don't like the songs they sing."

"Not I," purred the cat. "I'm prioritizing my life."

"Very well then, I will teach them myself," said the Little Red Hen. Carefully she prepared each week's lesson, collected yarn for craft time, discipled the mare and kept up with her daily chores.

Soon the Little Red Hen was running to and fro like a chicken with its . . . like the very busy chicken she was, when the doorbell rang. It was Mrs. Goose from across the courtyard, who was in charge of the piglet nursery.

"I don't see how I can possibly do another thing," sighed the Little Red Hen.

"But if you don't, we'll have to endure the grunting of so many little piglets in the worship service."

"We can't have that," said the Little Red Hen. "If I can't find someone to help, I'll do it."

By now the Little Red Hen was all but losing her sanctification toward the others, and the tone of her voice nearly scared one of the cat's lives completely out of her.

"Who will help in the nursery this week?" yelled the Little Red Hen.

"Not I," said the pig. "I am doing the Scripture reading."

"Not I," intoned the duck. "I have special music

during the offertory."

"Not I," mewed the cat. "I am allergic to the filthy things."

"Very well," said the Little Red Hen. "I will do it myself."

Sunday afternoon came, and the Little Red Hen was lying in a heap on the kitchen floor, suffering from severe burnout. She was so exhausted she could not rise to make dinner for the household.

She heard a knock at the door and raised her head just in time to see the mare, her pastor and Mrs. Goose bringing a plate of fresh bread, hot corn on the cob and an apple pie.

"This is for your hard work and diligence," the three said. "You have been such an encouragement to us that we wanted to encourage you." And with that they left as quickly as they had come.

The cat, the duck and the pig appeared at the window, sniffing at the air hungrily.

"Who will help me eat my dinner?" asked the Little Red Hen.

"I will," grunted the pig.

"I will," quacked the duck.

"I'd rather have tuna, but I guess I will," purred the cat.

"I followed up the decision card," said the Little Red Hen. "I taught Sunday school, and I helped out with the piglets in nursery. You three recited verses, sang and lay in the sun while I kept busy."

"Aw, come on, Little Red Hen," the pig said. "You know we're not as mature as you. Have a heart. We've learned our lesson." The duck and cat agreed.

"If I didn't care for you I would gladly offer you an equal portion of my bounty," the Little Red Hen said. "However, I do care and wish you to change your behavior."

And the Little Red Hen practiced tough love that day and ate the bread, the corn and the pie all by herself.

BEAUTY & THE
MARK OF THE BEAST

nce upon a time there was a sweet-dispositioned young girl named Beauty who followed all the passing fads in her Christian world. At this point in her life she was very much into angels. She had figurines by her bedside, pictures of angels on her walls and bookshelves filled with angel tomes from every publisher under the sun.

Her father was a wealthy, respected merchant and a member in good standing with the Believer's Business Men's Committee. He read all the current books about excellence and believed success followed the committed Christian wherever he went.

Alas, when Beauty began buying golden angel earrings and necklaces with ruby seraphs, his fortune was soon lost, and he could not bring himself to go to the meetings.

One day word arrived that a sailing vessel filled with his multilevel sales products had come to port, and he was filled with great hopes of returning to his upper-middle-class lifestyle.

"What would you like me to bring back to you, Beauty?" her father asked.

"Only yourself, Father," she replied. "And maybe a book about the end times. I think prophecy is going to heat up again, so I'd better read up on it."

When he reached the port and located his ship, he set up meetings and asked everyone to list three things they've always dreamed of owning. However, he could sell none of the merchandise and failed to recruit any local distributors, so he junked the ship and declared bankruptcy. For him it truly was an economic earthquake. Realizing he would never be asked to speak at a success seminar, he dejectedly made his way home.

In the deep forest he lost his way in a furious thunderstorm. In a flash of lightning, he was relieved to spy a mansion on a nearby hilltop. When no one answered his knock at the door, he pushed it open, calling, "Hello? I'm a financially challenged entrepreneur on his way home, and I'm in need of shelter."

Not a soul came, so he helped himself to dinner. When he finished he went upstairs to thank the generous host. He found not a living soul, but in a guest room he discovered a budgeting guide and a newsletter detailing the latest investment strategies. On the other side of the room he was amazed to see an entire wall of shelves filled with hundreds of books about eschatology. There were numerous books on the Second Coming and the tribulation period, along with posters of the rapture.

He found a book with an angel pictured on the front and picked it from the shelf. When he turned to leave, he heard a terrifying shriek, and a hideous figure stood before him. The man wore a polyester suit, and a pocket protector protruded from his shirt. He was balding but had combed his thin hair forward from the back.

"You ungrateful guest! How dare you!" the man roared. "After I give you food and shelter and some budgeting tips, you steal from my most prized possession? I just knew it would come to this. The signs are everywhere."

"I did not know," said the father. "I am a poor merchant and was only taking this home for my beautiful daughter, who expressed interest in eschatological things."

"Is she a New Ager?" asked the man.

"Of course not; she's a very devout young lady."

"Is she a member of the Trilateral Commission?"

"Certainly not," the father answered. "Her hobby is angels, and she buys many trinkets."

"Well, if you're so destitute, how does she purchase them?" asked the man.

"I am sorry to say she charges them."

Again the man shrieked and covered his face. "Don't you know the credit card is the precursor to the mark? First came MasterCard, then the bar codes. Tomorrow they come for me."

"I promise to cut them in half as soon as I return home, but please let me take this book to my daughter."

"If she really wants to read it, let her come here," said the owner. "But if you do not bring her back, I'll know you're part of the Illuminati."

Beauty's father returned home and explained the problem. She consented to go with him to the castle, spend some days in fellowship with its owner and prove she knew nothing of these conspiracies.

When they walked in, Beauty was listening to a contemporary song about angels on her headset. The man shrieked, "Subliminal messages!"

Those first few days were quite tenuous for Beauty and the homeowner, but they made it through. Beauty read more and more about prophecy and made plans to attend several conferences. Gradually her love grew for the man in polyester, but there were still many communication problems. When they argued the man shrieked like a wild animal, and that is why Beauty called him "the Beast."

"Beast," she said one day affectionately, "I've been down to the bookstore and have purchased several titles about relationships. Don't you think we need to improve our communication?"

"What do you mean?" said the Beast.

"Well, you're a microwave and I'm a crock pot. You think visually and I think with my emotions."

"I don't think we have a problem," said the Beast.

"Denial ain't just a river in Egypt," she said.

So they stopped discussing the ashes of the red heifer and focused on word pictures. "Let me understand what you're saying," the Beast learned to say. And then he would state his version of what she had said.

As they grew to accept each other's flaws, Beauty discovered she was falling in love with the Beast. They went through many hours of premarital counseling and a couples' retreat before they wed.

As a shared hobby they took up the study of temperaments and discovered Beauty was a "phlegmatic/cocker spaniel" and the Beast was a "melancollie."

As they had more and more children, Beauty and the Beast began to focus on their family. They went through many books on the strong-willed child and found out that parenting isn't for cowards. They learned not to make idle threats about punishment and instituted a time-out rule.

The Beast, a firstborn, sang choruses at men's retreats while Beauty immersed herself in Christian romance novels. Their love was strong and took them through many other prevailing trends in the subculture.

However, Beauty never did get over her fascination with angels and credit cards. And the Beast, though he worked on his tone of voice, remained quite loud. It's sad to say, but after the birth of each child he crept into the nursery and checked under the bonnet of his new baby for any sign of a beastly mark.

In spite of all their foibles and fads, the two lived relatively happily ever after.

RUMPELBOOKSELLER

 very poor but sincere Christian speaker/author traveled with his daughter, who sang, played the piano and had a badly produced CD. Because of his desire to reach more people with his message, he went to speak with a publisher. Losing his head in the process, he told the editorial committee that his daughter had the ability to spin gold out of overstocked books.

"That's quite a spiritual gift," the editors said. "If your daughter is that clever, bring her to the warehouse tomorrow so we may put her to the test."

This vexed the daughter mightily, because she wasn't even able to sell her own CDs, let alone unsold books. But after throwing a tantrum, she consented to help her distressed father.

When the girl arrived the next day, they led her into a room full of biographies by professional athletes and recording artists.

"Now set to work," they requested, "and if by early morning you have not changed these books into money, we won't give your father a contract."

So the poor pastor's daughter was left alone. She had no idea what to do, and her heart ached so much that she began to weep.

Suddenly she heard a noise at the window. When she opened it, in leaped a small man who was—well, to be kind, not a looker. He was not gifted with height, and he grinned from ear to ear.

"What's the matter with you?" he said.

"I am a poor piano player who can't even sell my own music, and my father has promised I can sell these books by morning. It's hopeless."

"I can do it," said the man.

"What's it going to cost me?"

"Your piano will do," he answered.

As soon as the girl agreed, he picked up the phone and made a quick demographic survey, fired off a few direct fax appeals and spun his sales with lightning speed. The girl fell asleep in the corner, and when she woke up the man was gone. To her amazement, so were all the books.

At sunrise the editors came and rejoiced at the girl's work, for they were very conscious of their inventory. They took her to a warehouse that was twice the size of the first room and said, "If you can move these, we'll even publish your father's novel."

When the door had been shut and locked, the girl saw that the room was filled with biographies of older sports stars with bad knees who had become singers. It was a very difficult lot.

The girl slumped into despair once more—but soon she heard a familiar sound at the window. In popped the little man, with the same grin on his face.

"Before you begin," she said, "I have nothing left to pay you. The piano was my treasure, but it is yours."

"Then you must promise me the first royalty check and the advance from the sale of your father's first parenting book."

That sounded quite reasonable to the girl, but then the man added, "Plus you must promise me your first-born child."

Well, who knows whether I will ever have a child at all?

thought the girl. Since she had no alternative and figured she could bring a lawsuit if necessary, she promised the man what he desired.

Immediately he began spinning the books to potential buyers. He booked three cruises filled with fans of aged singing sports stars and a boat full of gerontologists. By the next morning all the books were gone.

When the editors arrived, they were quite happy and offered her father a contract on the spot.

Not long after that the girl married, and a year later she had a wonderful child. The infant had a high Apgar score and was teething with molars by its first birthday. By this time the girl's father's fame had grown, for his teaching truly was sound. He had his own radio program, a newsletter and three bestsellers, and his first book on parenting was due in the fall. Having learned from his previous mistakes, he passed along great parenting wisdom to his daughter.

Just before the child's birthday party began, the girl heard a sound at her window. When she opened it, she found the smiling little man.

"What do you want?" she asked.

"I have come for my due," he said. "You promised

the advance and first royalty check from your father's book."

The daughter was terrified, because she knew he would ask for the child next. "How about giving me three days and letting me guess your name?"

"Are you kidding?" said the man. "A deal's a deal. Hand over the money, and don't forget to include the baby."

With the child wailing in the background, the girl began to smile. The wisdom imparted by her father was about to pay off. "OK," she said, "but if you take the money and the child, you have to keep them. Return one and you lose rights to the other."

The little man agreed, and the girl made him sign his name—which proved to be Rumpelbookseller—on a hastily drawn contract of her own. He took the royalty check and the child and disappeared through the window.

However, diaper changing, midnight feedings, teething pain, constant crying, formula mixing and added laundry soon brought the little man to the realization that being a full-time mom is a lot like spinning straw into gold. It's hard work, and you get no recognition from society.

He returned the next day with bloodshot eyes. "I

can't take it anymore," he said, and handed over the child and the check. It was the first time the girl had seen Rumpelbookseller without a smile on his face. And she has never heard from him since.

HANSEL & GRETEL

ear a great forest there lived a poor cutter of wood whose company was downsizing because of a family of spotted owls. He and his wife were in the sandwich years and worried not only about their two children but also about their aging parents. The children, Hansel and Gretel, were both home-schooled.

Since school vouchers were not available, the parents had no control over their educational dollars. They were heavily taxed by the current administration and could afford only a small house in a shabby neighborhood. They had a compact car, rarely went out to eat and had to settle for basic cable, no premium channels.

One fitful night the father lay in bed thinking, turning and tossing. His resolve for home-schooling was waning under the intense financial pressure. Finally he said to his wife, "What will become of us? If you don't go out into the workplace and bring in another income, we won't be able to afford a bigger house."

"Maybe you can get a second job," she replied. "Can't you become more than a carpenter?"

"I am stretched to the limit," he said. "I think I have repetitive stress syndrome as it is."

"We can't afford to send the children to a Christian school," answered the wife. "If I am to go out, we will have to send them to public school, and we will need a second car."

"It will be a great sacrifice," the husband said, "but I will take public transportation and you can have the car."

"Agreed," said the wife. "Early in the morning we will provide Hansel and Gretel with their lunch. We will take them to the schoolyard and leave them until late in the afternoon."

"But wife," said the man, "if we leave them in such an environment, the secular humanists may devour their little minds. Outcome-based education could scar them forever. It may be increasingly difficult to pass along our values, and perhaps the two will grow up unable to distinguish right from wrong."

"But," she countered, "if we keep home-schooling and I do not find a job, we'll stay in this dingy home with its one-car garage the rest of our lives."

"Good point," he said. "I'm probably overreacting. Besides, there's always quality time."

The walls were so thin in the house that Hansel and Gretel had heard every word. Gretel began to cry.

"Don't worry, Gretel," Hansel said. "I have a plan."

The next morning the mother said, "Rise and shine, children; we have a special field trip planned. It's social interaction day, and you're going to meet many new friends." When Hansel and Gretel did not get up, their mother counted to three several times. Finally they dragged themselves out of bed and got dressed.

As the family walked along toward school, Hansel tore pieces from his low-cholesterol peanut-butter-and-jelly sandwich and dropped them on the ground.

When they reached the playground, the father and mother patted their heads and bid them goodby.

"Rest yourselves here, children," he said. "Mother

and I will come back for you soon. If we're not back by three-thirty, take the bus."

So Hansel and Gretel sat by the swingset and had an early lunch while they watched the other children play. When the bell called the schoolchildren inside, the two followed the sandwich trail home. There they whiled away the hours singing along with their audiotape collection until their parents returned.

The next day the parents returned them to the school with money for a hot lunch. This time Hansel pulled offering envelopes from his pocket and dropped them at intervals along the road. (Hansel scribbled on these each Sunday morning and had quite a collection.)

But Hansel ran out of envelopes while they were still a good way from the school, and when they were ready to go home they were unable to find the trail. So they wandered the school hallways until they saw a cheery classroom decorated with colorful drawings. A middle-aged woman came to the door and beckoned them inside.

"Come," she said, "we are beginning the first chapter in our new reader, *Heather Has Lots of Cousins, Too.*"

Gretel sat at the back of the class and watched the

children misspell words while Hansel went to the reading circle. "This is whole language, deary," the teacher whispered to her. Then she wrote on Gretel's slate, "I no ure gong to luv it."

Later, when the bus dropped Hansel and Gretel at home, the father and mother greeted their children and debriefed them.

"What was the best part of your day, Gretel?" asked her mother.

"I liked the spelling bee," she said.

"Did you win?" the father said, for he was very grade-conscious.

"Of course not," said Gretel. "There are no winners or losers. We all received ribbons for participation, because competition damages the psyches of those who are alphabetically challenged."

"I see," said her mother. "What did you learn today, Hansel?"

"In science I learned I am only a little more advanced than animals. We have all been taught our parents' myths about religion and life. But best of all, I came to understand why you and Father sent us to the wonderful new school."

"And why is that?" asked his father.

"We played a game called Lifeboat," he said. "And

now I understand that Gretel and I are simply learning to swim."

So Hansel and Gretel tried their best to adapt to their new surroundings. The family did move up to a four-bedroom bungalow with a two-car garage and pool in the back. They upgraded their cable subscription and ate dinner out more often. But the parents were so busy they had little time to ponder the effects of their commitment to income-based education.

THE FISHERMAN & HIS CONGREGATION

 faithful pastor who tried hard to keep his work and family life balanced loved to fish on his day off. The stroll to the lake and the fresh air made him forget the weight and worry of his small congregation. Though he loved to fish, he rarely caught anything.

One beautiful Monday morning he baited his hook and cast it far into the lake. Immediately he felt a strong tug and reeled in an enormous fish. But before he could take the hook out, the fish looked at him and said, "Pray let me live, good sir. I am really an enchanted man formerly known as a prince; I only appear to be a Northern Pike. Put me back in the water and let me go."

"I could never hurt a talking fish," the pastor said. "Swim away in peace." So the fish left him.

At the board meeting the next day the pastor said, "What a grand fish I caught yesterday. He said he was an enchanted prince."

"What did you do with him?" asked the head of the board.

"I threw him back," replied the pastor.

"You didn't ask him for anything?"

"No. What should I have asked for?"

"Ah," groaned the deacon. "We worship in this hovel of a church with leaky pipes and a hissing radiator. Our nursery is musty, we have no kitchen to speak of, and our songbooks are falling apart. Go back and tell the fish we want a beautiful sanctuary and some new hymnals."

The pastor did not like the idea, but he was terrified of the leadership of the church. So he stood at the water's edge and called,

"O fish that I caught,
I'm in water that's hot.
There's none in the nation
Like my congregation
That sends me to beg of thee."

The fish came swimming to him and asked, "What does your congregation want?"

"They say I should have asked you for a new sanctuary and, if you could spare them, some nice new hymnals to replace the old ones."

"Go back to the church then," said the fish. "They are in the sanctuary already."

When he returned he saw huge stained-glass windows, a fountain flowing from the baptistery and sparkling red hymnals in the racks on the back of each cushioned pew.

Everyone was quite pleased for about a week. After the service the next Sunday, the pastor was greeting people when a member whispered in his ear, "The sermons you give are not seeker-friendly."

"And what would you have me to do?" asked the pastor.

"Go back to the fish and ask him for a new computer and a CD/ROM version of *Complete Pastoral Stories and Illustrations for the Unchurched,*" said the member.

Though he hated asking the fish for another favor, the pastor went back and called out toward the water,

"O fish that I caught,

I'm in water that's hot.

There are constant frustrations
With my illustrations,
So they've sent me again to thee."
"What is it this time?" asked the fish.

"I need to be more seeker-friendly so that we might bring more unchurched into the services," said the pastor. "Could you possibly spare a few multimedia aids that might bring my technique up to speed?"

"Very well," said the fish. "Your new computer is already there, and the software is preloaded."

The following Sunday the pastor's message was "Fifteen Minutes to an Eternal Relationship." The sermon was well received because it was filled with stories, illustrations and pop culture allusions, and, of course, it lasted only fifteen minutes.

All went well until Wednesday night, when several urgent personal needs were brought to the pastor's attention.

"We need you to counsel these individuals and help them overcome their problems," one elder said.

"How can I spend time with my seeker-friendly message, get the church's administrative work done, be a good husband and father, and still counsel all these by myself?" the poor pastor asked.

"We'll send you to a men's conference next year

with thousands of others who are in their warrior stage," said the elder. "For right now go tell the fish to make you a good counselor."

The fish was waiting at the edge of the water with his fin on his chin. "Back so soon?" he said.

"Yes, my church wants my total commitment to counsel our members," the pastor said. "My days are filled with message preparation, administrative chores and visitation, and they still want me to be God's man in the family with perfect children and a Proverbs 31 wife."

"Have you been to any men's conferences?" said the fish.

"I'm supposed to go next year," answered the pastor.

"Until then, I've provided you with Micro-Psych, the new Windows counseling software, and your wife can now accompany you on the piano."

The pastor returned home and found these improvements. He also discovered that both his children suddenly had beautiful smiles and could recite numerous memory verses through their pearly white teeth.

Alas, the congregation still was not happy.

"We want to be the number-one church," said a

member who was very into church growth statistics. "My research shows we can achieve a 300 percent growth spurt with a new gymnasium, professional musicians, lasers, a five-state bus ministry and a drive-in theater that broadcasts our service from a huge parking lot."

"Don't you think that's a bit much?" asked the pastor. "We're having a hard time keeping track of all the people as it is. Plus, how could we take an offering with all those people at the drive-in?"

"Haven't you ever heard of in-line skates?" asked the member. "It's a perfect ministry for our teens."

Though he tried, the pastor could not talk the church out of sending him to the fish again.

"O fish in the lake,
You may think me a flake
To ask for a union
With a skating communion,
But they say we'll be number one."

"Let me guess," said the fish. "Church growth?"

"How did you know?" said the pastor.

"I saw some of your members fishing yesterday in a stream north of here that's lined with willows. It's a very nice creek, but it's a mistake to make it run through your particular church setting."

"I wish I could convince them otherwise," said the pastor.

So the fish gave them all they asked, and the church became number one in the entire kingdom. Articles were published about it in major news magazines. But with all their success, the people of the congregation couldn't sleep for thinking what they could do next.

A group of concerned members gathered one morning for breakfast and decided to ask for a king to be appointed from the church who would have absolute rule.

"Can't we be content with being number one?" said the pastor. "We had twenty-five thousand people last weekend!" But the members would not relent.

As he approached the lake, black clouds gathered and thunder roared overhead. Lightning flashed, and the fish appeared on the water. The pastor trembled before him.

"They want a king," said the pastor.

"A king?" said the fish. "Go back to them and rejoice, because they have needed this all along."

When the pastor returned, he was astonished. The stained glass was gone. The buses, the parking lot, the theater screen, the gymnasium and most of the people were gone too. In their place, restored to its original condition, was their little church.

Today the congregation worships there in humility. Every time they sing from their battered hymnals or hear the leaky radiator clang, they thank the true King for their pastor and promise not to ask so much of him ever again.

THE EMPEROR'S
NEW BIBLE

any years ago there lived an Emperor who cared much for the outer things of man. He loved good food, fine clothes and a steady coach that got many miles per slave. He also loved to accumulate Bibles, though he did not spend much time reading them. He kept them hidden in his innermost chamber and admired them each night before going to bed.

One day two unsavory characters arrived in his great city and proclaimed themselves translators of Holy Writ. Hearing of their expertise, the Emperor had them brought to his royal chambers.

"I have many translations, amplifications, paraphrases and commentaries," the Emperor said. "I have a One-Year Bible, a One-Week Bible, a One-Minute Bible for People on the Go and a Thirty-Second Bible for People on the Go with Incredibly Small Attention Spans. Can you possibly give me anything new?"

"We can, Your Majesty," the wily thieves said. "We have been reimagining a translation that will delight all those who are righteous and inclusive in their language. Those who understand intellectual things will find this work unique in all the world. Those who do not are simply not very spiritual. Alas, all we need are the funds to get a committee together."

So the Emperors gave the two rascals a wad of cash, and they began work at once. The two demanded the richest ink and the oldest manuscripts. Valuable heirlooms were brought to them at a moment's notice and were never seen again.

I should like to know how far they have gotten, thought the Emperor one day. But he was afraid that among the committee's elite minds he might not understand the translation and thus would prove himself to be unspiritual. "I will send my honest Minister of Theology to the translators," he thought.

The Minister of Theology, a long-nosed gentleman

with great bushy eyebrows, walked into the hall. The two men were scribbling the following words on the royal blackboard:

Philippians 4:13: I can do all things through my own efforts, because the Lord helps those who help themselves.

"Mercy preserve us!" said the Minister of Theology. "You've changed the entire verse."

"We don't want religion to be a crutch," said the men. "People should stop believing fables and take responsibility for their lives."

The Minister went closer and found that all masculine references to God were changed from "He" to "He/She" and, where appropriate, to "The Eternal It."

Can I indeed be unspiritual? thought the Minister. *Not a soul must know I cannot see the sense of this translation.* So the Minister of Theology left the men and gave a fine report to the Emperor.

The thieves asked for more money to help in their work. This time the Emperor sent it along with an honest statesman who was a member of the Emperor's yearly prayer breakfast.

"Look at our latest translations," the men said when the statesman entered the hall.

On the blackboard he saw the following verse.

Romans 3:23: For all have made negative choices in their lives and are not living up to their own expectations.

"We have changed the Romans Road to the Romans Path to Peace and Prosperity," said the men. And they pointed to the next verse, which read thus:

Romans 6:23: The payment for negative choices in life is low self-esteem, but the gift of The Eternal It is self-fulfillment in all you do. You deserve a break.

The statesman was aghast at what he saw, yet he did not want anyone thinking him unspiritual or opposed to scholarly pursuits. He too gave a good report to the Emperor.

All the people of the town were talking about the new Bible. Animal rights activists were overjoyed that Old Testament sacrifices were being changed to tree-planting ceremonies. Feminists who had long complained to the Emperor about the authoritarian nature of the Scriptures were delighted in the translation of 1 Timothy 2:12: "I do not permit a woman to teach or to have authority over a man, unless she really feels like it."

All references to sin were plucked out. All references to hell were supplanted with positive statements of God's love. The new Scriptures did not banish the unregenerate to outer darkness but affirmed "everyone who is really sincere in their belief system."

The miracles of Jesus were gone. References to Lazarus's rising from the dead and to Jesus' resurrection were deleted so as not to offend those who were resurrection-impaired.

At last the scoundrels bound their slim-line work with an attractive leather cover and presented it to the Emperor. He was so thrilled with the job they had done that he said, "I'll give you something extra if you'll prepare an Emperor's Study Edition. I would also love for you to take a look at our hymnal. It seems so outdated by comparison." The two accepted gladly.

The Emperor's counselors suggested that he sponsor a public reading of the text for the entire kingdom. "What a splendid idea," he said, and a great procession was held in honor of the completed work.

The royal orator produced the meager text with a flourish and began to read from Genesis. "In the beginning," he read, "and over billions of years and much evolution, The Eternal It created heaven and earth." The footnotes pointed out that the Bible is not a textbook and the original creation account was simply metaphorical.

Particularly well received were the stories of Noah and the local flood, Moses and the Ten Suggestions, and the survival of the three Hebrew children who were thrown into a hot tub at Nebuchadnezzar's spa.

When the orator made it to the New Testament, Jesus had very little to say. The flawed account of Judas was changed because he was, after all, simply a financial opportunist working within his own moral frame of reference.

The crowd cheered the reading. The Emperor applauded. But on the edge of the square sat a small child who listened intently to the words. Finally he could take it no longer and cried out above the din, "The Emperor has no Bible! These are not the words I have been taught."

A murmur went through the crowd. One whispered to another what the child had said. "The lad is right," said a father. "These are not the words of our Lord."

The Emperor, who had been heeding the excellent delivery of the orator and not the content, approached the lad. "You are questioning the work done on the texts?" he said.

"Your Majesty," answered the boy, "if you will but

read from my Bible and compare the words, you will understand."

The boy pulled a shabby old book from his pocket and handed it to the Emperor. "For the wages of sin is death," the Emperor read, "but the gift of God is eternal life in Christ Jesus our Lord."

Upon reading the text the ruler suddenly felt naked before the crowd. It was the first time he had read these words as anything but literature. He grabbed the new translation and tore it in half, then commanded that the scoundrels be thrown from the kingdom.

Through the faithful witness of one small boy, the Emperor was saved from spiritual ruin. And from that day forward the Emperor did not merely collect God's Word but began reading it, living it and hiding it in his heart, which he found to be much better than keeping it on his bedroom shelf.

THE PIED PIPER
OF FIRST CHURCH

here is a tiny village near you named Hamelin, and most of the residents attend First Church and many sing in the choir. The Melody River runs by the town's southern wall and continues through less quaint towns.

Not too long ago the people of Hamelin were having an awful time. The problem was music! The choir sang great hymns of the faith with much breath support and stunning arrangements. But the baby boomers wanted more contemporary tunes with guitars and synthesizers. The children were too young to understand and were content to sing "Jesus Loves Me."

The clamor between the two factions became so great that a delegation from each group met the church staff in the pastor's study.

"Why can't we hear our kind of music in the service?" cried the boomers. "We want relevance. We want something with a little life and a beat so we can invite our friends."

"Why should we get rid of our great heritage for some praise choruses?" said the choir director. "Your friends don't need sugarcoated lyrics, they need substance."

On and on the argument went, until there was a knock at the door. A cheerful voice drawled, "May I come in?"

"Enter," said the exasperated pastor. The man who entered looked quite odd. He was tall and fit, for he used the latest Christian exercise videos regularly. Under his arm he carried an electric guitar, and behind him he pulled a roadcase containing synthesizers and effects boxes.

"Sir," he said to the pastor, "I have an answer to your musical problem. I'm often called on to rid a community of vermin, snakes, ants and people of the older demographic. But in this case I believe I can soothe both factions in your church and teach them eternal things as well."

"What is your name?" the pastor asked.

"I used to be known as the Pied Piper," the man said. "Of course my pipe is digitally sampled now, but you can't go around as the Pied Keyboardist or the Pied Lead Guitarist, so I'm sticking with Piper."

"What will it cost us?" asked a staff member on the finance board.

"This gig will be difficult, but we can talk about royalties and residuals later," the Piper replied. "First let me show you what I can do."

The group watched in amazement as the Piper plugged his guitar into an amplifier, opened his road-case and began wailing strains of a contemporary "Amazing Grace."

Footsteps pounded through the church hallway, and an army of youngsters crowded around the study. Baby boomers shoved and leaped over one another to get close to the sound. The steeple rocked and the church bells chimed as the drum machine banged out its rhythm.

The young crowd was overjoyed to hear music that spoke to their souls. But the old guard was not impressed. "If this is your answer to our problem," said one, "we'll take our choir to another church."

"Not so fast," said the Piper. He pulled a synthesizer from his roadcase and played the same song with the beautiful sounds of a pipe organ. The music filled the study and could not be contained by the massive sanctuary. Hymn lovers were overcome with the majesty of the sound and thanked the Piper profusely. Some even thought of clapping but restrained themselves.

The Piper then set up music workshops and trained the most talented youngsters in the arts of writing and composing. It wasn't long before they were taking texts from established hymns and singing new songs.

For the choir, the Piper brought out original manuscripts of the classics. They sang with great fervor and enjoyed the Piper's knowledge of their kind of music.

When the Piper finished his final seminar, he asked for payment. Unfortunately, he did this the first Sunday of combined contemporary and traditional worship.

"Payment?" screamed the choir director. "You have ruined our service! Certainly you have appeased the younger generation with their guitars and gospel songs, but you have done something far worse. You have legitimized their musical form. We will not give you a penny."

"I am not in the mood to dicker," the Piper said. "I've been called by a prominent science periodical to rid them of some pesky creationists. It's time to pay the Piper. You won't like what happens if you don't."

"We do appreciate all you've done here," said the pastor in a conciliatory tone. "But I think we'll handle things ourselves from now on. We've invited a boomer specialist to come in next week and straighten out the kids."

"Then you leave me no alternative," said the Piper. He pulled a strange machine from his case and turned it on. A loud buzz filled the church, and the congregation looked in amazement as hymnals and sheet music disappeared. Guitars, synthesizers and even the massive pipe organ were sucked into the machine, never to be heard again.

In addition, each member lost the ability to distinguish one note from another. On that day not one person could sing a tune or even hum in the shower. Songbirds around the church flew from their nests, and the halls fell silent.

The Piper took his machine to the river and pitched all the notes and chords, all the time signatures, the instruments, the choir robes and the piano into the deep stream.

"You have no right to take our music away," said one choir member in a rather monotone voice. "If we'd known you were going to do this we would gladly have sung a praise chorus or two."

"That's right," agreed a baby boomer. "And we would sing some of those old hymns if we could have our music back. They weren't that bad."

But it was too late. As much as the congregation wished for another chance, the Piper had taken their music from them forever.

There remains one ray of hope for First Church, however. If you listen closely, among the shaking rattles and chimes of mobiles, you may hear the faintest strains of "Jesus Loves Me" coming from the nursery.

KING MIDAS &
THE CHRISTIAN TOUCH

ome time ago there lived a king named Midas who was very wealthy and quite concerned about the encroachment of the pluralistic society on his kingdom. He spent much of his time fighting for prayer in the schools. Curiously, however, he very seldom prayed with his lovely daughter, Christiana.

While the hot sun beat down in the afternoon, Christiana would play in the vineyard while King Midas thought about ways to reverse the culture's dreadful trend toward secularism.

"Please read to me," said Christiana one day. She loved to hear Mother Goose rhymes, and because the king could not think of a Christian alternative, he took up the book and recited "Jack and Jill."

At the part where Jack fell down, a thought came to him: *If only everything in my kingdom could become Christian, the world would be a much better place. The world would be safe for my daughter, and I wouldn't have to worry about lawsuits, unless of course it was a Christian world that didn't read the Bible very carefully.*

"If only I could have the power to make everything Christian," he said aloud. "I would give anything to have that power, anything at all."

As he stared into space as fathers sometimes do, Christiana said, "Come on, Dad, read!"

But her pleas fell on deaf ears, for all at once King Midas was stunned by a bright light and a piercing voice that said, "Your wish has been granted, King Midas. As soon as the sun rises tomorrow, anything you touch will become Christian."

"Will it change into a deeply committed Christian thing or simply become lukewarm?" King Midas asked.

"That is for you to see," said the voice—which being interpreted means, "It's for me to know and you to find out."

And find out he did. In the morning King Midas

awoke fitfully from sleep and found the mattress he was lying on had become Christian. The tag displayed the manufacturer's name with addresses in Wheaton, Illinois, and Colorado Springs, Colorado.

Anything I touch now will become Christian, thought the king. *How wonderful for me and all my kingdom.*

Immediately he jumped out of bed and put on his shoes, which became sandals. He ran down the stairway eagerly, looking for objects to touch, and came upon his daughter's book of nursery rhymes. One touch, and instantly the book was transformed! Every story, every poem, now had a religious slant.

The king ran on to one of his favorite places, the royal baseball diamond. Players for the minor-league Nuggets were running wind sprints and chewing tobacco, which should be done only by professionals.

Forgetting his gift, King Midas approached a particularly rugged player who was the star of the team. Upon seeing the king the slugger uttered a few unprintable words and offered his hand.

Instantly the chaw in his cheek and his stubbly beard disappeared. "Praise the Lord," he said to the king. "It's a real blessing to meet you."

I've never heard this player talk this way in postgame interviews, the king thought. Aloud he said, "You are certainly a talented young man."

"Well, I just want to thank the good Lord," the player said.

King Midas was overjoyed about the effect he was having on his kingdom. He ran into a royal used-car lot and leaned against one of the automobiles to catch his breath. Straightaway, each end of the car was graced with bumper stickers that said "One Way" and "Honk If You Love Jesus."

King Midas then stepped into the dealer's office and shook hands with the owner and his sales staff. They too turned Christian and began praising the Lord by offering markdowns on their inventory.

The king walked by the royal broadcasting center with its radio and television outlets and thought, *Why not?* Thus it came to be that one minute his kingdom was watching a talk show that paraded people with every known relational dysfunction across the screen. The next minute they were watching the same people being counseled by a Christian psychologist/faith healer.

King Midas was not only delighted in the change, he was ecstatic that all he had to do was touch a person or object to make it holy. No hard work, no prayer, no long days of waiting and struggling. Just a little touch, and each thing or person was converted.

Walking back toward the palace, he touched flowers and trees, which thereupon sprouted "Jesus Loves Me" buds. He met the gardener, an unkempt, bushy-haired individual with a long beard. When King Midas touched him, his hair turned three different shades of orange, and he went running toward the nearest televised sporting event to hold up a "John 3:16" sign.

The king approached two children who were playing with violent action toys. One touch, and the toys became biblical violent action toys with spears and slingshots.

A group of concerned politicians had gathered by the palace. When King Midas shook hands with them, they turned from the opposition party to the "League of Believers," a new Christian coalition.

King Midas knew he had one important person left to touch. He found Christiana alone by the grapevines, reading her new Mother Goose book. He touched her gently on the cheek and watched closely to observe the metamorphosis.

To his surprise, he did not see any change. So he touched her shoulder a bit more firmly.

"What are you doing, Father?" she asked.

"I'm trying to turn you into a Christian," he said, and grabbed her arm and shook it vigorously.

"Father," she said meekly, "since my youth I have known of the things of God, as the Sunday-school teachers have taught me. The words from the book about the man from Galilee, his perfect life, his perfect sacrifice and the forgiveness he offers—that message touched my heart long ago."

"Then I have been misled," said the king. "I have thought all this time that I was making a society Christian. But you are saying it is not true. The voice I heard must have been lying."

"The only One who can truly change our culture and the people in it is the One who touches the heart," Christiana said with wisdom beyond her years. "You certainly have affected the outward appearance of men, such as the baseball player and the used-car salesman. But tomorrow one will put cork in his bat and the other will overcharge his customers for a brake job unless the Spirit reaches them."

King Midas looked sad, and teardrops fell down his cheeks like so many little fish symbols. He loved his daughter even more because of the valuable lesson he had learned.

From that day forward he and Christiana devoted

themselves to prayer for the kingdom. They regularly visited the poor, the widows and the orphans and set up a shelter for the homeless. They related the timeless message that the Great King of Glory loves people and wants them to know him. One by one people's lives were changed, and the kingdom was never the same.